Camp Kayak Adventures!

Greetings Young Reader!

Welcome to the first book in the Camp Kayak series!
My love for reading and writing was instilled into me
by my loving mother who was a very inspiring English teacher.
As a child, I remember listening to and enjoying what
I affectionately call "front porch tales" being told by my grandparents
and parents on their front porches on cool breezy nights.

My son has shared his front porch tales with me too, and I'm excited
to bring those stories to life through children's books.
Now, sit back, kick up your feet, and let's go on an adventure!

Sincerely,
Hillivi McDonald

Hillivi McDonald

Mrs. Carson Swallows a *Fly*
a Camp Kayak Adventure

illustrated by Imoian Press

Nayberry Publications, Opelika, AL

Copyright 2010 by Hillivi McDonald
Illustrations copyright @ 2010 by Hillivi McDonald

Published in the United States by Nayberry Publications for Kids
a division of Nayberry Publications, Opelika, AL

www.nayberrypublications.com/kids
www.campkayakadventures.com

Educators and librarians, for a variety of teaching tools visit us at
www.campkayakadventures.com

Library of Congress Cataloging-in-Publication Data
McDonald, Hillivi
LCCN: 2010941632

ISBN 13: 978-0981584355
ISBN 10: 0981584357

Printed in the United State of America
1

Tweet, tweet… tweet, tweet.
The Blue Jays chirped sweetly as the morning
sun peeped through BJ's bedroom window
and warmed his sleepy face.

1

"BJ, it's time to get out of bed. Breakfast is waiting and it's the first day of summer camp," mom called gently.
"Coming mom," BJ moaned, as he hopped off the bed wondering if he would like summer camp. Down the stairs he strolled into the kitchen to join his sister Jade at the breakfast table.

3

HONK, HONK, HONK!
The camp van **had arrived**. Mr. Toler the driver
was a jolly, **bald** guy who waved as Jade and BJ trotted
toward the van. "Bye mom", BJ sighed, wishing he could stay
home with her. Dad gave him the "**thumbs up**" sign as the van
pulled away. Jade never noticed **her** parents waving
because she was too busy talking with Ashley.
They've best friends since Kindergarten.

7

Inside Building B kids were seated at tables by their age group. Jade and Ashley ran to the 8-year-old table as BJ edged toward the 10-year-old table with a frown on his face. He didn't look around to see if he knew anyone. He didn't even care! His stomach just turned upside down as he put his head down on the table.

As she began to call the names on her list, BJ crossed his fingers and held his head down. With her huge voice she called the group members' names loud and clear. BJ thought he was safe but, when she got near the end of her list she called out BJ. BJ's legs became stiff. He couldn't move. Beams of sweat popped from his forehead. He couldn't believe his counselor was none other than

MRS. CARSON!

14

ROOM - 33

Mrs. Carson walked like a proud peacock as she led the students to Room 33. She had everyone an assigned seat and there were tons of arts and crafts materials at each table. But before they were allowed touch anything, she went over the summer camp rules and made everyone introduce themselves.
"RATS!"
BJ said as he fretted about standing up to introduce himself in front of the other students.

16

Mr. Smith then grabbed her from behind and pushed her stomach in two times but nothing happened! She just kept gagging and wheezing and hacking. By this time, Mr. Finnie rushed in and swung Mr. Smith out of the way. He gave her one GREAT push with so much FORCE, the fly plopped out of her mouth and into her coffee cup.

21

ROOM - 33

Camp Kay

Mrs. Carson slowly peeled herself from the table. She snatched her purse off the teacher's desk. She squared her shoulders and marched out of the classroom door, clutching her neck. Mrs. Carson left for the rest of the day and Mr. Smith took over the class. He announced that he would be in our class to help Mrs. Carson for the summer. This was great news because Mr. Smith is exciting too. He even took us for a boat ride after lunch!

23

By the end of the day BJ had three new buddies. He was just as excited as his sister Jade as they boarded the camp van to go home. BJ could not wait to get home to tell his parents about his first day at summer camp and what happened to weird Mrs. Carson. He still couldn't believe she had swallowed a fly!

24

At dinner, BJ was the "chatter box!"
He told his parents all about Mrs. Carson's mishap,
his new buddies and his boat ride after lunch. His parents
were so glad he had a good day at summer camp. Of
course, Jade wanted to share her day's adventure
but BJ's story about Mrs. Carson seemed
more interesting.

25

www.ingramcontent.com/pod-product-compliance
Lightning Source LLC
Chambersburg PA
CBHW041006170626
46815CB00002B/180